THE
Baby's
Good Morning Book

KAY CHORAO

E. P. Dutton   New York

The author and publisher believe that the necessary permissions have been obtained and are acknowledged on the facing page. In the event any questions arise as to the use of any material, the author and publisher express regret for any error inadvertently made and will be pleased to make the necessary corrections in future editions of this book.

Library of Congress Cataloging-in-Publication Data
Chorao, Kay.
    The baby's good morning book.

    Includes index.
    Summary: A selection of poems and rhymes by a
variety of English and American poets.

    1. Children's poetry, American.   2. Children's
poetry, English.   3. Nursery rhymes.   [1. American
poetry—Collections.   2. English poetry—Collections.
3. Nursery rhymes]   I. Title.
PR1175.3.C47   1986   821'.008'09282   86-6415
ISBN 0-525-44257-X

Published in the United States by E. P. Dutton,
2 Park Avenue, New York, N.Y. 10016
Published simultaneously in Canada by
Fitzhenry & Whiteside Limited, Toronto
Editor: Ann Durell   Designer: Riki Levinson
Printed in Hong Kong by South China Printing Co.
First Edition   COBE   10 9 8 7 6 5 4 3 2 1

ACKNOWLEDGMENTS

The author and publisher gratefully acknowledge permission to reprint on:

page 13, "Will There Really Be a Morning?" by Emily Dickinson, from *The Poems of Emily Dickinson,* edited by Thomas H. Johnson, published by Little, Brown and Company.

pages 18 & 19, "Ducks at Dawn" by James S. Tippett from *Crickety Cricket: The Best-Loved Poems of James S. Tippett.* Copyright 1933 by Harper & Row, Publishers, Inc. Reprinted by permission of Harper & Row, Publishers, Inc.

page 20, "Getting Out of Bed" by Eleanor Farjeon. From *Eleanor Farjeon's Poems for Children* (J. B. Lippincott Co.). Copyright 1933, 1961 by Eleanor Farjeon. Reprinted by permission of Harper & Row, Publishers, Inc. And from *Silver Sand and Snow,* published by Michael Joseph Ltd.

page 25, "Singing-Time" from *The Fairy Green* by Rose Fyleman. Copyright 1923 by George H. Doran Co. Reprinted by permission of Doubleday & Company, Inc., and The Society of Authors as the literary representative of the Estate of Rose Fyleman.

page 27, "Sunrise" from *City Sandwich* by Frank Asch. Copyright © 1978 by Frank Asch. By permission of Greenwillow Books, a Division of William Morrow & Company.

page 32, "That May Morning" from *Is Somewhere Always Far Away?* by Leland B. Jacobs. Copyright © 1967 by Leland B. Jacobs. Reprinted by permission of Holt, Rinehart and Winston, Publishers.

page 52, "Twinkletoes" from *When We Were Very Young* by A. A. Milne. Copyright 1924 by E. P. Dutton, renewed 1952 by A. A. Milne. Reprinted by permission of the publishers: E. P. Dutton, a division of New American Library, and Methuen Children's Books.

page 54, "I Am Rose" by Gertrude Stein, from *The World Is Round,* © 1966, Addison-Wesley, Reading, Massachusetts. Poem. Reprinted with permission.

This book belongs to

_____

Contents

Time To Rise

by Robert Louis Stevenson

A birdie with a yellow bill
Hopped upon the windowsill,
Cocked his shining eye and said:
"Ain't you 'shamed, you sleepyhead!"

Will There Really Be a Morning?

by Emily Dickinson

Will there really be a morning?
Is there such a thing as day?
Could I see it from the mountains
If I were as tall as they?

Has it feet like water-lilies?
Has it feathers like a bird?
Is it brought from famous countries
Of which I have never heard?

Oh, some scholar! Oh, some sailor!
Oh, some wise man from the skies!
Please to tell a little pilgrim
Where the place called morning lies!

A Dewdrop

Little drop of dew,
Like a gem you are;
I believe that you
Must have been a star.

When the day is bright,
On the grass you lie.
Tell me then, at night
Are you in the sky?

Elsie Marley

Elsie Marley is grown so fine,
She won't get up to feed the swine,
But lies in bed till eight or nine.
Lazy Elsie Marley.

Ducks at Dawn

by James S. Tippett

"Quack! Quack!"   "Quack! Quack!" they said.
Said seven ducks at dawn   "It's time to eat.
While night dew   We'll go hunt mushrooms
Glimmered on the lawn.   For a treat."

And in the light
Of early dawn
I saw them chasing
On the lawn.

They sought their treat
With hungry quacks
And marked the dew
With criss-cross tracks.

They ate the mushrooms
One by one
And quacked to greet
The rising sun.

But in my bed
I settled back
And slept to tunes
Of "Quack! Quack! Quack!"

Getting Out of Bed

by Eleanor Farjeon

Up with you, lazybones!
Over the brink!
Don't stop to pick up heart,
Don't stop to think,

Don't stop for *any*thing!
Jump out of bed,
Gather your garments
Wherever they're shed.

The chair has your stocking,
The table your vest,
Your shoe's in the fender,
Your shirt's on the chest,

Your belt's on the door-knob,
And you are in bed;
Wake yourself, shake yourself,
Up, sleepy head!

The Year's at the Spring

by Robert Browning

The year's at the spring,

And day's at the morn;

Morning's at seven;

The hillside's dew-pearled;

The lark's on the wing;

The snail's on the thorn:

God's in his heaven—

All's right with the world!

Singing-Time

by Rose Fyleman

I wake in the morning early
And always, the very first thing,
I poke out my head and I sit up in bed
And I sing and I sing and I sing.

Sunrise

by Frank Asch

The city YAWNS
And rubs its eyes,
Like baking bread
Begins to rise.

Morning Is a Little Lass

by Frances Frost

Morning is a little lass,
Her gay head yellow-curled,
Who jumps a rope of knotted flowers
Across the waking world.

29

Little Bird

Once I saw a little bird
　　Come hop, hop, hop.
And I cried, "Little Bird,
　　Will you stop, stop, stop?"

I was going to the window
   To say "How do you do?"
But he shook his little tail,
   And away he flew.

That May Morning

by Leland B. Jacobs

That May morning—very early—
As I walked the city street,
Not a single store was open
Any customer to greet.

That May morning—it was early—
As I walked the avenue,
I could stop and stare and window-shop,
And hear the pigeons coo.

Early, early that May morning
I could skip and jump and run
And make shadows on the sidewalk,
Not disturbing anyone.

All the windows, all the lamp posts,
Every leaf on every tree
That was growing through the sidewalk
Seemed to be there just for me.

Towards Babylon

Little lad, little lad,
  Where were you born?
Far off in Lancashire,
  Under a thorn,
Where they sup buttermilk
  With a ram's horn
And a pumpkin scooped
  With a yellow rim
Is the bonny bowl
  They breakfast in.

Jemima

There was a little girl, and she wore a little curl
  Right down the middle of her forehead.
When she was good, she was very, very good,
  But when she was bad, she was horrid!

One day she went upstairs, while her parents, unawares,
  In the kitchen down below were occupied with meals,
And she stood upon her head, on her little truckle bed,
  And she then began hurraying with her heels.

Her mother heard the noise and thought it was the boys
  A-playing at a combat in the attic,
But when she climbed the stair and saw Jemima there,
  She took and she did whip her most emphatic.

The Pancake

by Christina Rossetti

Mix a pancake,
Stir a pancake,
    Pop it in the pan;
Fry the pancake,
Toss the pancake—
    Catch it if you can.

One Misty, Moisty Morning

One misty, moisty morning,
    When cloudy was the weather,
I chanced to meet an old man,
    Clothed all in leather.

He began to compliment,
  And I began to grin.
"How do you do?" "And how do you do?"
  "And how do you do again?"

Ten o'Clock Scholar

A diller, a dollar,
A ten o'clock scholar,
What makes you come so soon?
You used to come at ten o'clock,
But now you come at noon.

The Violet

by William Wordsworth

A violet by a mossy stone
Half hidden from the eye!
—Fair as a star, when only one
Is shining in the sky.

Hark, Hark

Hark, hark,
The dogs do bark;
The beggars are coming to town:
Some in rags,
And some in jags,
And one in a velvet gown.

The Worm

by Ralph Bergengren

When the earth is turned in spring
The worms are fat as anything.

And birds come flying all around
To eat the worms right off the ground.

They like worms just as much as I
Like bread and milk and apple pie.

And once, when I was very young,
I put a worm right on my tongue.

I didn't like the taste a bit,
And so I didn't swallow it.

But oh, it makes my mother squirm
Because she *thinks* I ate that worm!

49

The Silent Snake

The birds go fluttering in the air,
    The rabbits run and skip,
Brown squirrels race along the bough,
    The mayflies rise and dip;
But whilst these creatures play and leap,
The silent snake goes *creepy-creep!*

The birdies sing and whistle loud,
    The busy insects hum,
The squirrels chat, the frogs say "Croak!"
    But the snake is always dumb.
With not a sound, through grasses deep,
The silent snake goes *creepy-creep!*

Twinkletoes

by A. A. Milne

When the sun
Shines through the leaves of the apple-tree,
When the sun
Makes shadows of the leaves of the apple-tree,
Then I pass
On the grass
From one leaf to another,
From one leaf to its brother
Tip-toe, tip-toe!
Here I go!

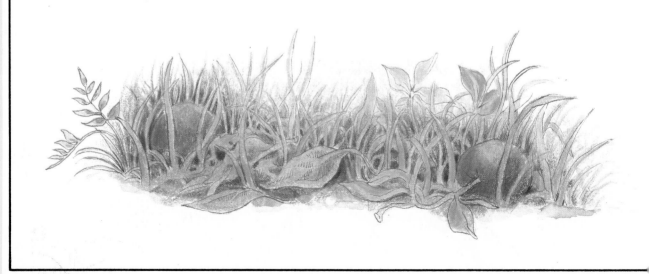

I Am Rose

by Gertrude Stein

I am Rose my eyes are blue
I am Rose and who are you?
I am Rose and when I sing
I am Rose like anything.

The Crocus

by Walter Crane

The golden crocus reaches up
To catch a sunbeam in her cup.

I'm Glad the Sky Is Painted Blue

I'm glad the sky is painted blue,
   And the earth is painted green,
With such a lot of nice fresh air
   All sandwiched in between.

Happy Thought

by Robert Louis Stevenson

The world is so full
    of a number of things,
I'm sure we should all
    be as happy as kings.

Index of first lines